LEGO® STAR WARS™

OFFICIAL LEGO® STAR WARS™ ANNUAL 2016

A LONG TIME AGO IN A GALAXY FAR, FAR AWAY . . . .

Good and evil existed in the universe long before the Force was discovered. Now, evil is rearing its ugly head again. The Jedi Knights are the galaxy's only hope – brave guardians gifted with the Force who defend peace with their lightsabers. A mighty Jedi starship is roaming the galaxy in search of the evil Sith. Can you put the missing pieces back in the right places? Write the number of the correct piece in each gap.
Be careful, there's one piece you don't need.

1
2
3
4
5
6

THE POWER OF THE LIGHT SIDE

The evil Sith set an explosive trap for the Jedi Masters! Thanks to their sensitivity to the Force, Kit Fisto, Obi-Wan Kenobi and Mace Windu sensed the trap before they reached it. Lead them through the corridors to their ship, so they can avoid the blast!

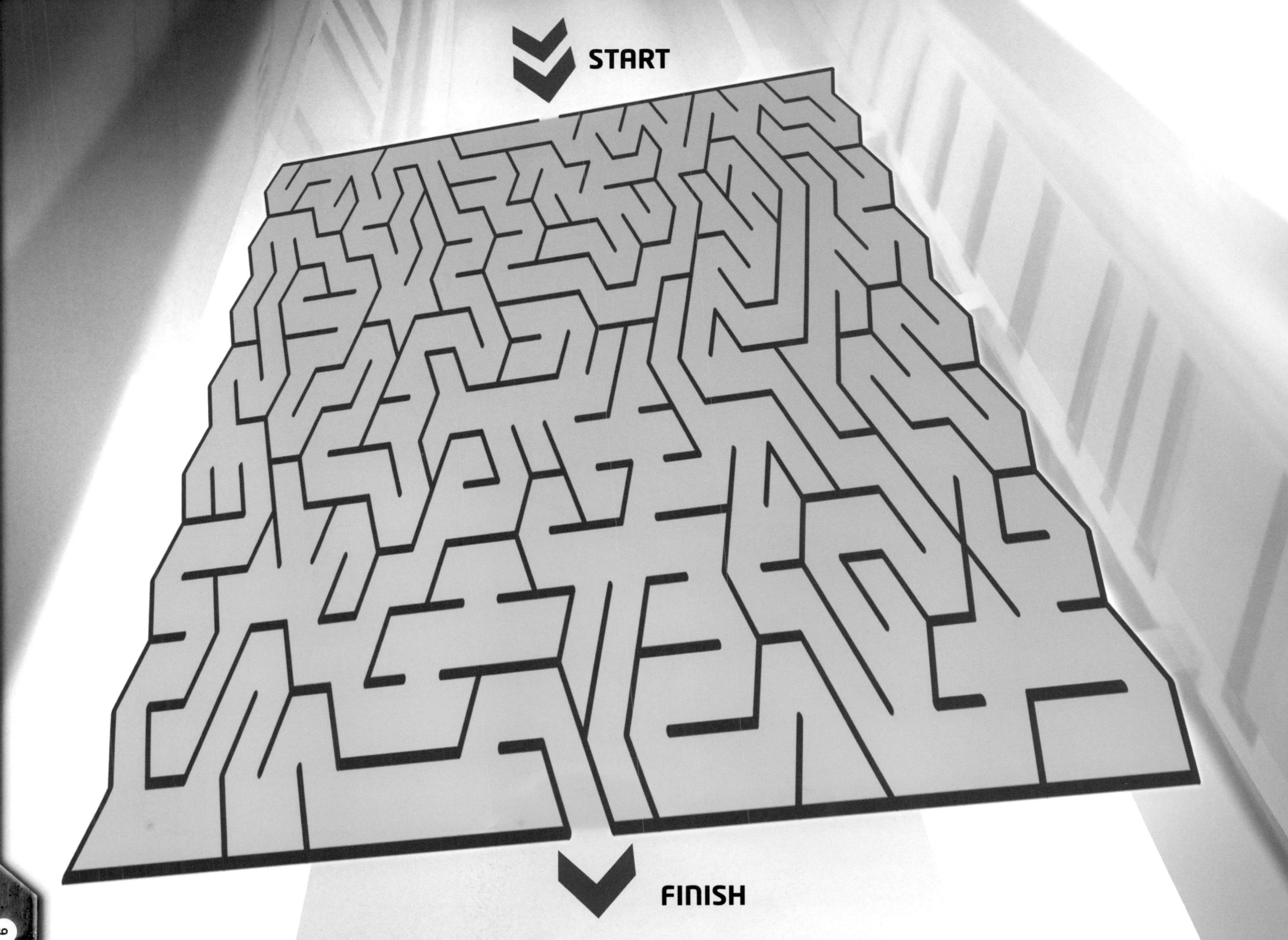
START
FINISH

GOLDEN-MOUTHED DROID

The Droids' Spelling Bee Championship is about to end. Help C-3PO win first prize – use lines to connect the letters and spell the words below. Remember, each letter can be used only once.

A
C
L
H
O
O
E
R
A
C
C
O
B
H

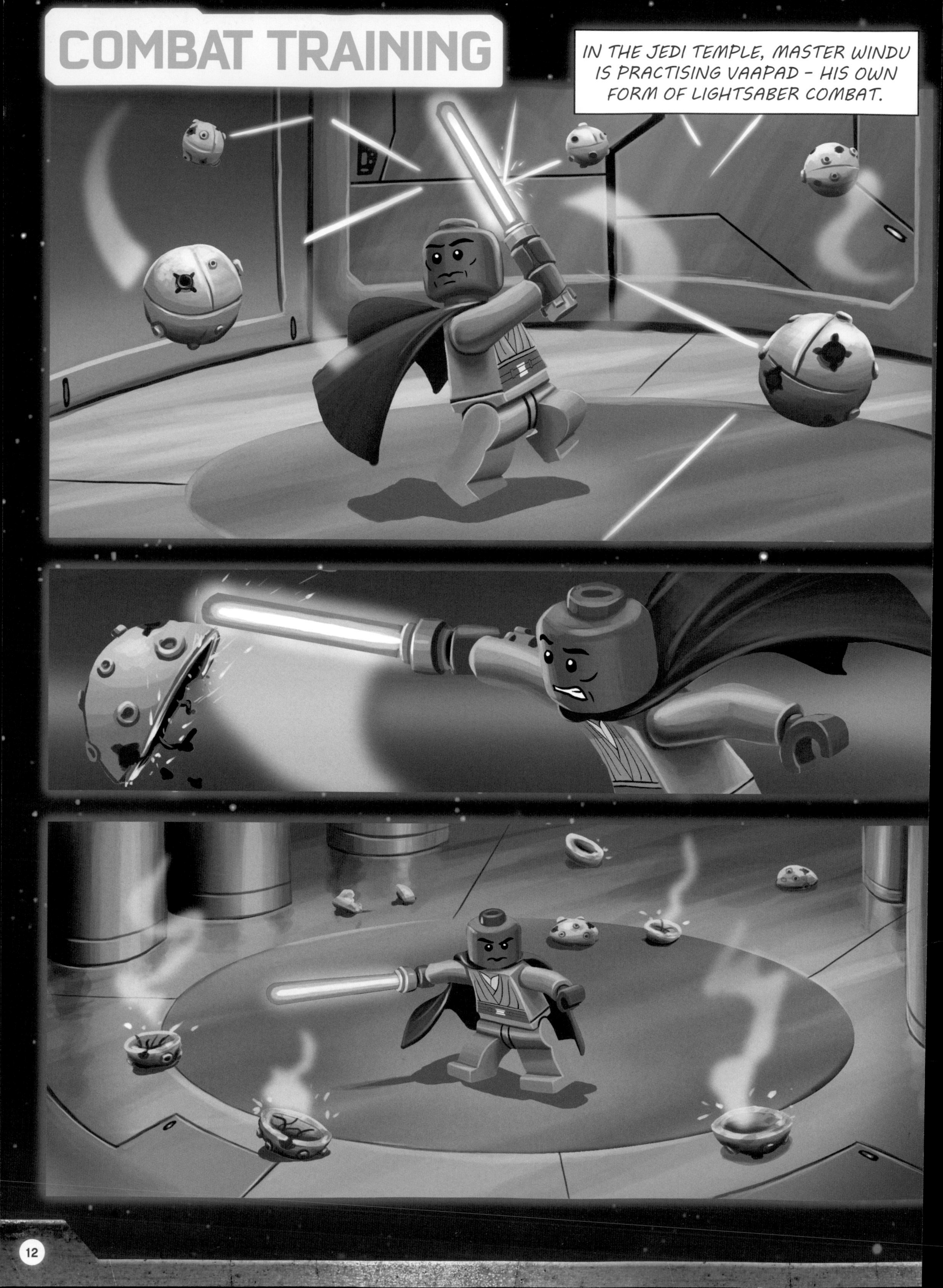
COMBAT TRAINING
IN THE JEDI TEMPLE, MASTER WINDU IS PRACTISING VAAPAD - HIS OWN FORM OF LIGHTSABER COMBAT.

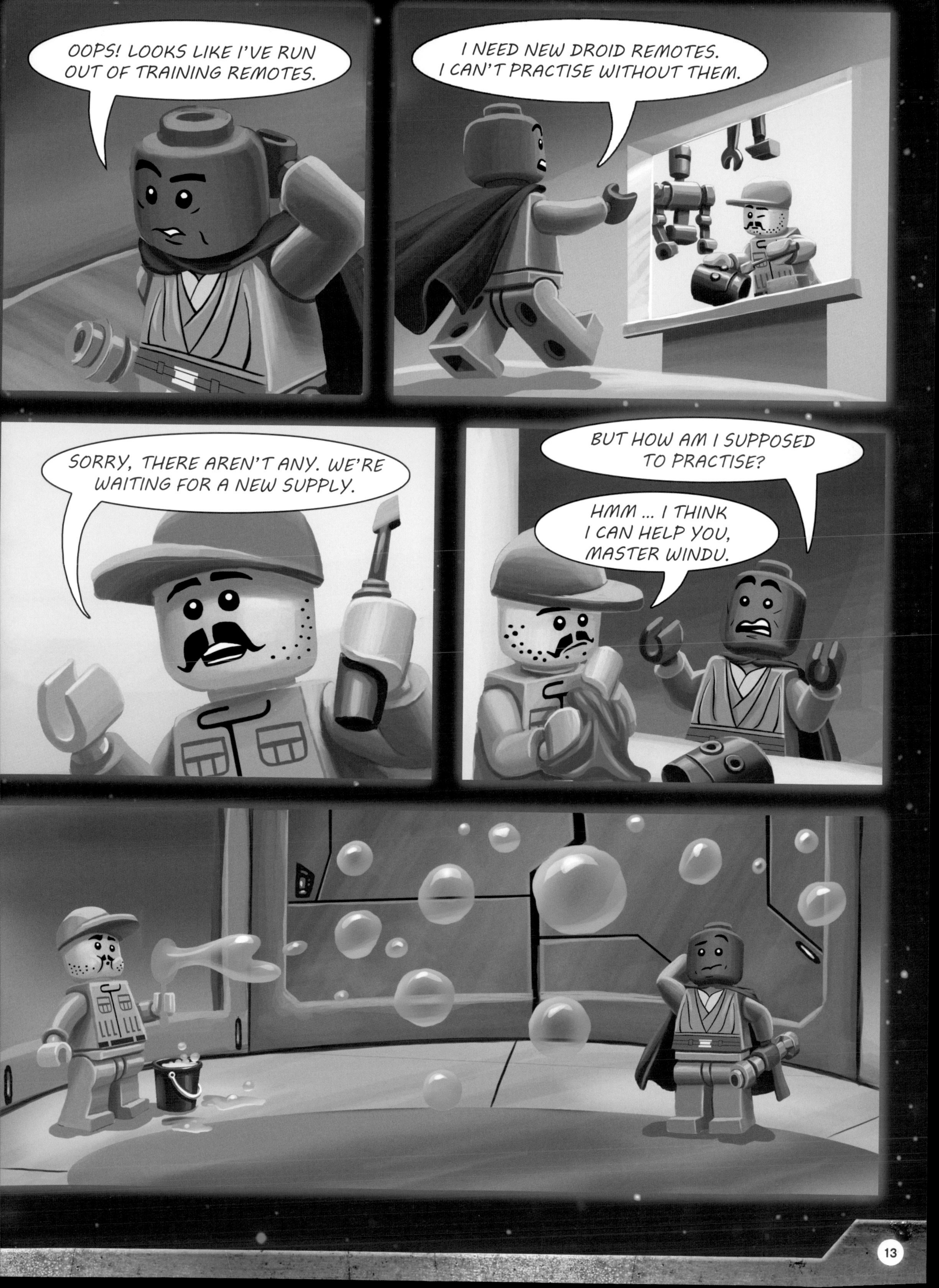
OOPS! LOOKS LIKE I'VE RUN OUT OF TRAINING REMOTES.
I NEED NEW DROID REMOTES. I CAN'T PRACTISE WITHOUT THEM.
SORRY, THERE AREN'T ANY. WE'RE WAITING FOR A NEW SUPPLY.
BUT HOW AM I SUPPOSED TO PRACTISE?
HMM ... I THINK I CAN HELP YOU, MASTER WINDU.

THE SEARCH

Young Force users are detected by the midi-chlorian count in their blood. The higher the count, the stronger the Force is in them. Add up the numbers and work out which young Jedi Academy student has the greatest potential. Write the total for each student in the empty space next to their box.

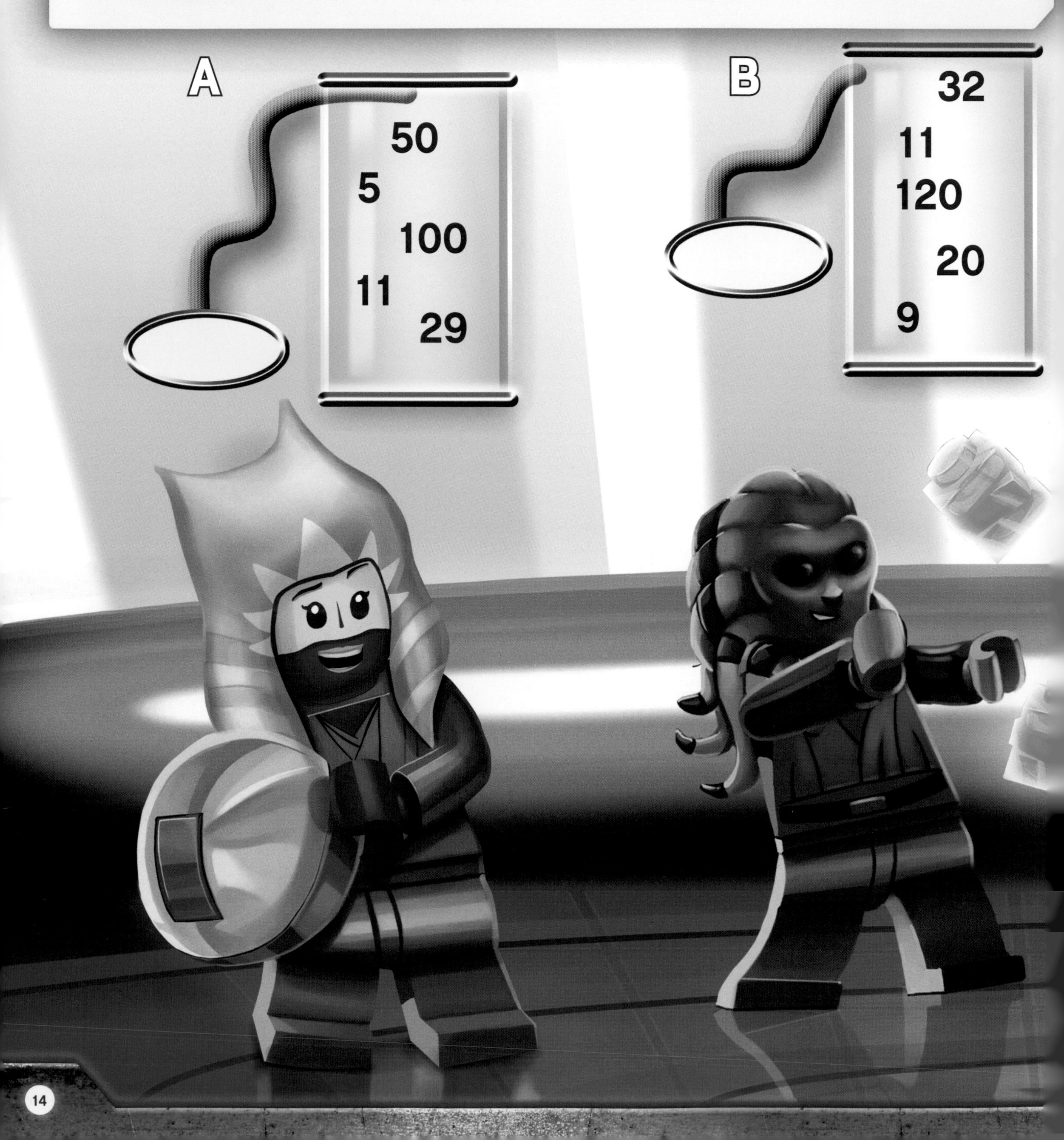

C
15
80
34
22
19
D
140
35
60
18
5
BOBBY

A NEW CAREER

Jabba the Hutt wants to start breeding banthas, but before he can set up his new business, he needs to get a good price for some banthas. Look closely at the grid and count how many times the word BANTHA appears – then you'll know how many Jabba bought.

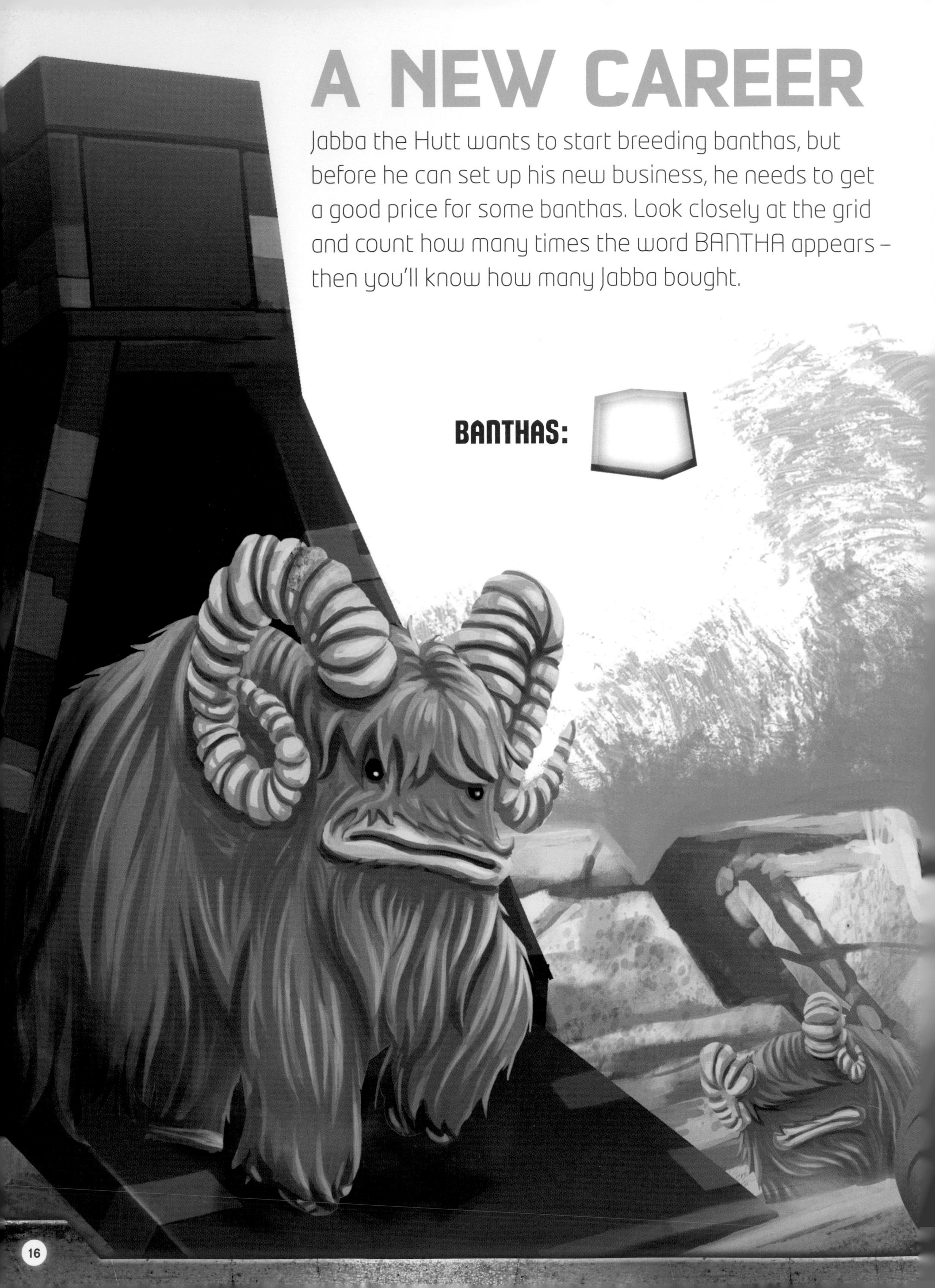

BANTHAS:

B A A N T A B A N T T A
A B A N T H A B A N A T
H A B A B B A N T H A H
T A B A T N A N A B A N
B A N T H A B H A T A N
A B B A N A T H A B A N
B A N T A B A N T H A B
T A B A N T H A B A A N

JEDI MASTER

Master Yoda is a powerful Jedi who leads the entire Jedi Order. Although he is small and calm, he's an expert warrior who wields a mighty Force! Use your own powers to work out which of the smaller mirror images of Master Yoda opposite matches the larger image on this page.

1

2

3

4

5

6

LOST IN THE BOG

Obi-Wan Kenobi and Yoda got lost on a marshy planet while they were searching for the Sith. Obi-Wan is beginning to worry, but Yoda seems to know the way. Lead the Jedi Masters through the marshes to their ship.

START
FINISH

FIGHT FOR THE GALAXY

For centuries the Sith have tried to take over the galaxy. Fortunately, thanks to Jedi Knights and Republic soldiers, they have been unable to achieve their goal. Look closely at the space battle between the two forces and find the five ships shown in the smaller pictures.

JEDI ACADEMY

At the Jedi Academy, students train to become Jedi Knights. They are taught how to be good, fight with a lightsaber, pilot starships and, most importantly, how to use the Force.

Master Yoda often spends time solving riddles with his pupils in class. Test your powers – see if you can work out the answers to these riddles.

What stops a tauntaun rider from sitting on his mount?

The saddle.

What's so sensitive it disappears even when you whisper?

Silence.

What's the best place to learn how to swim?

Water.

You can hear it, but can't see it;
you feel it, but can't catch it;
some say it's good, others say it's bad.
What is it?

The wind.

QUI-GON JINN'S DISCOVERY

On the planet Tatooine the Jedi Knight Qui-Gon Jinn finds a young boy with an incredibly high midi-chlorian count. Is this boy, named Anakin Skywalker, the Chosen One who will bring balance to the Force? Study the picture of Anakin below, then help the Jedi find the real boy among the look-alikes opposite.

1
2
3
4
5
6

SITH SCHEMES

The Sith Lords will never stop trying to take control of the galaxy. The master and the apprentice don't trust anyone, not even each other. Which two small pictures don't appear in the big scene?

1 2 3 4 5 6

ON THE DARK SIDE

Anakin Skywalker has been tempted by the dark side of the Force! He'd better get used to wearing dark clothes, drinking black coffee and thinking about dark stuff then! Which dark shadow belongs to Anakin? Circle the correct one.

VADER'S PROBLEM
I MADE SURE THE BEST MEDICAL DROIDS IN THE GALAXY TOOK CARE OF HIM. WHY ISN'T HE HERE YET?

FIND HIM AND BRING HIM TO ME, RIGHT NOW!
YES, MY LORD!

I GAVE HIM UNLIMITED FUNDS FOR CLOTHES AND EQUIPMENT. WHERE IS HE?!

SOME TIME LATER ...
VADER IS IN HIS ROOM, MY LORD, BUT HE DOESN'T WANT TO COME OUT.
WHAT?

GO BACK TO VADER AND FIND OUT WHAT HIS PROBLEM IS!

MAYBE OBI-WAN HURT HIM AGAIN, AND HE'S RECOVERING?

15 MINUTES LATER ...
LORD VADER DIDN'T WANT TO TELL ME WHAT THE PROBLEM WAS, BUT HE PROMISES TO BE HERE AS SOON AS HE'S READY.

WHAT?

HMM . . . BLACK OR ORANGE?

GALACTIC CROSSWORD

Somebody has sent the Sith a crossword to solve, and the Emperor has nearly finished it. Why don't you have a go, too? The answers form a vertical word – it's the name of the planet where the Jedi Academy is found.

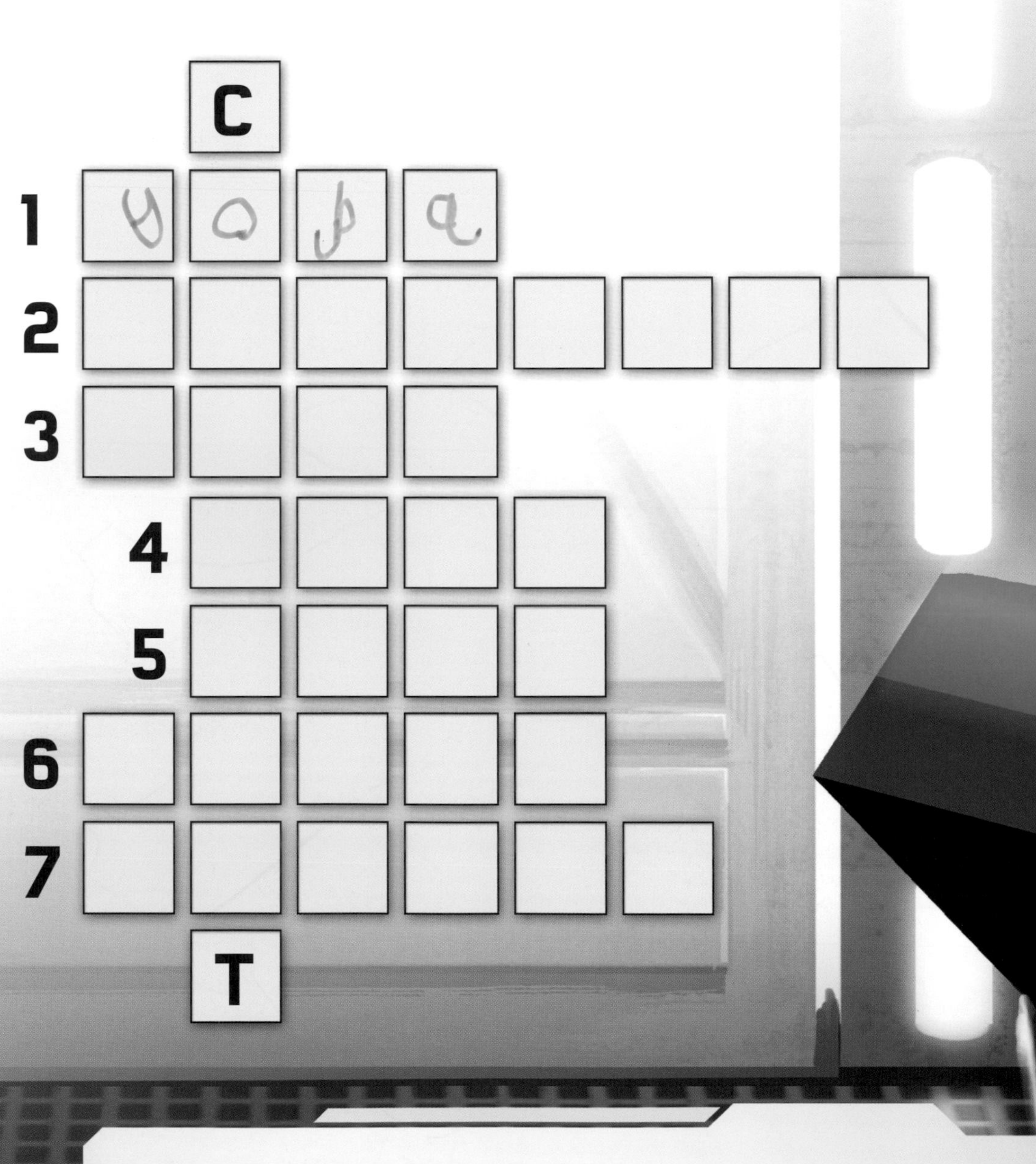

1. The short, green, Jedi Master.
2. The General who breathes heavily and collects Jedi lightsabers.
3. The species that the infamous Jabba belongs to.
4. The ones who want to gain control over the galaxy.
5. R2-D2's best friend.
6. The Dark Lord wearing a scary mask.
7. The one who was supposed to bring balance to the Force.

A DREAMER FROM TATOOINE

Luke Skywalker is a young boy whose biggest dream is to become a space pilot. Connect the dots and see which ship Luke would like to fly the most.

IMPERIAL DESTROYER

This machine is the most powerful ship in the galaxy, but it still needs fighters for protection. Count all the TIE fighters flying around the Star Destroyer and circle the correct number.

X-WING ATTACK

The X-wings launched an attack on the Death Star. Can the rebels destroy the enemy's superweapon? Lord Vader bet the Emperor three doughnuts that the rebels would lose! What do you think? While you're deciding, find 7 differences between the pictures.

HOTH BASE

The rebels built a secret base on the icy planet Hoth, so that they can hide from the Imperial forces. It's very cold, but Luke Skywalker and Han Solo are still enjoying themselves – they might even have a snowball fight and make a snowman if they have time ...

Suddenly the rebels see a wampa running off with a soldier. Quick! Catch the wampa before it eats the rebel for lunch! Lead Luke and Han through the maze, avoiding the snowdrifts, and save the poor soldier.

WAMPA
START

DANCING WITH THE STARS

At yesterday's party to celebrate the discovery of the rebel base on Hoth, Lord Vader showed off his best dance moves. Help him remember his routines – complete each dance sequence by writing the correct number in the empty box.

A
?

B
?

C
?

1
2
3
4

WEAPON SUDOKU

The conflict with the Empire is escalating! Now more than ever the rebels need a full armoury to fight the overpowering enemy forces. Add the missing weapons to the arsenal by writing the correct numbers in the empty spaces. Remember, each weapon can only appear once in each row and column.

BATTLE ON HOTH

A battle has broken out on the icy planet Hoth. Two rebel fighters are trying to stop an AT-AT – an Imperial war machine! Help Luke lead the snowspeeders straight to the AT-AT. Find a path through the maze of letters using only the squares marked 'AT-AT'. You can move only up, down or sideways across the grid.

START →	AT-AT	AA-TT	AT-YA	YY-TT	TT-AA	TA-TA	AT-YA	TT-AA
AA-TT	AT-AT	AT-YA	AT-AT	AT-AT	AT-AT	AY-TA	TA-TA	AA-TT
TA-TA	AT-AT	AT-AT	AT-AT	TA-TA	AT-AT	AA-TT	TA-TA	YY-TT
YY-TT	AA-TT	TA-TA	AY-TA	YY-TT	AT-AT	YY-TT	TT-AA	AY-TA
AY-TA	AT-AT	AT-AT	AT-AT	AT-AT	AT-AT	AT-YA	AA-TT	TA-TA
TA-TA	AT-AT	TT-AA	TT-AA	TA-TA	AA-TT	AT-YA	AY-TA	AT-YA
AT-YA	AT-AT	AT-AT	AT-AT	TA-TA	AT-AT	AT-AT	AT-AT	AA-TT
AA-TT	TT-AA	AA-TT	AT-AT	YY-TT	AT-AT	AY-TA	AT-AT	TA-TA
AY-TA	TA-TA	AT-YA	AT-AT	TA-TA	AT-AT	AA-TT	AT-AT	AT-AT
AA-TT	AT-YA	YY-TT	AT-AT	AT-AT	AT-AT	YY-TT	TT-AA	→ FINISH

THE BOUNTY BOUNCE

The bounty hunters are ready to serve the Empire – for the right price, of course. Match each dancing bounty hunter with the correct description and meet the cosmic rascals.

1
Despite this big helmet hiding my face, I see all and hear all.

2
I might look like a reptile, but I'm a great hunter.

BOBA FETT
BOSSK
3
I need a lot of oil to
keep myself from
creaking and rusting.
4
The white cloth on my
head hides mechanical
audio sensors.

A MESSY CANTEEN

Lord Vader loves order, and the dewback-riding stormtroopers have left a real mess in the canteen. They're in for a long clean-up! There's one thing missing from each of these four pictures – compare the pictures and mark the area where the item should be when you work out what it is.

VISIONS OF POWER

The Emperor is deciding what shape the new Death Star should be. Work out which piece fits where in the space station so that it matches Darth Sidious' vision. Write the correct numbers in the empty spaces.

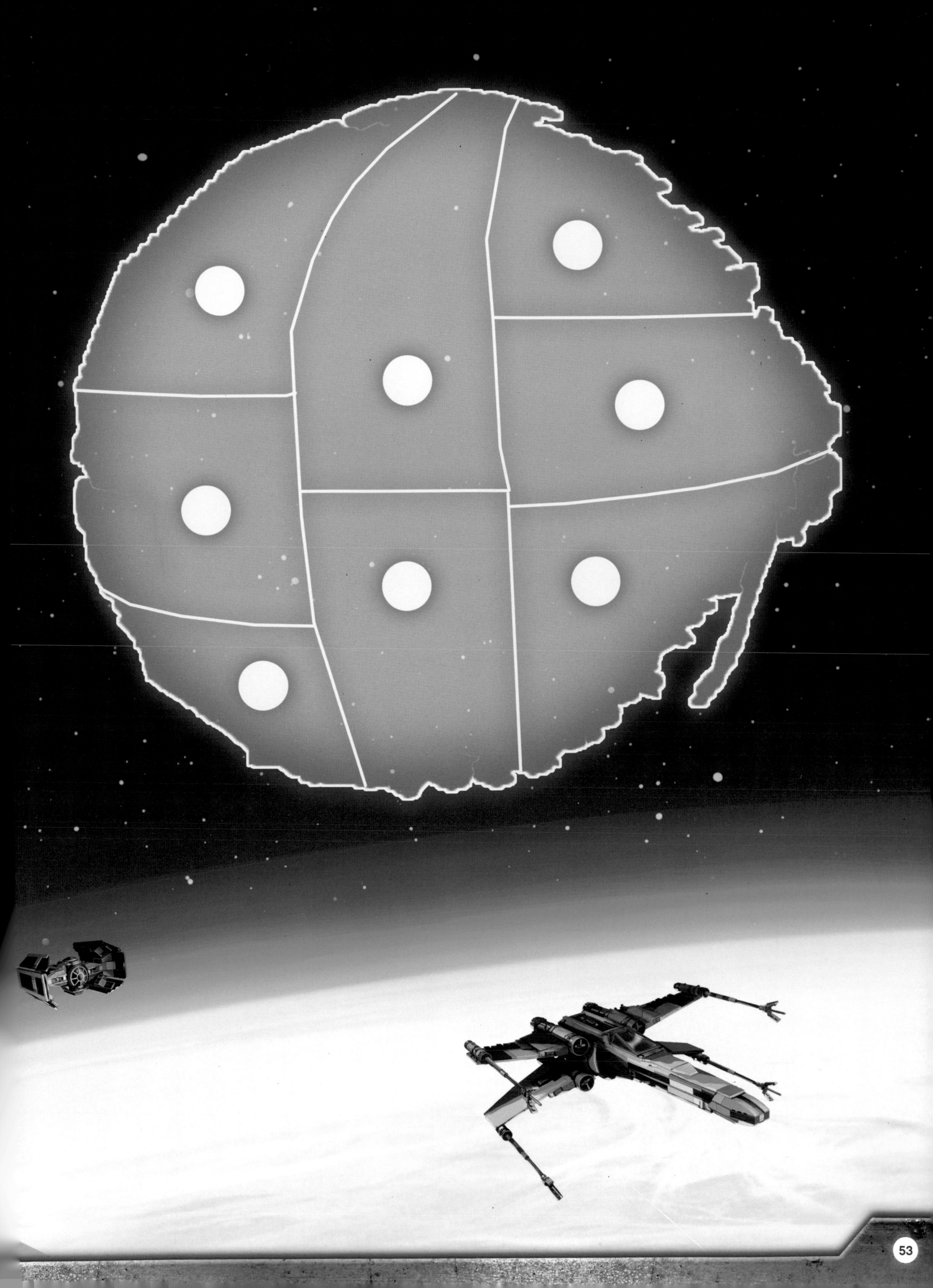

HIDDEN EWOKS

On one of Endor's moons, a tribe of brave Ewoks is helping the rebel commandos fight the Empire. How many Ewoks can you spot? Can you find 6 rebel commandos wearing green uniforms? There are also 2 little white droids in there – can you see them?

VICTORY

The rebels managed to destroy the second Death Star, and are hoping that the Emperor won't build a third! Look closely at the pictures on the next page and put them in order to watch the battle – number them from 1 to 4.

ANSWERS

Pg. 6–7
A LONG TIME AGO IN A GALAXY FAR, FAR AWAY . . . .

Pg. 8–9
THE POWER OF THE LIGHT SIDE

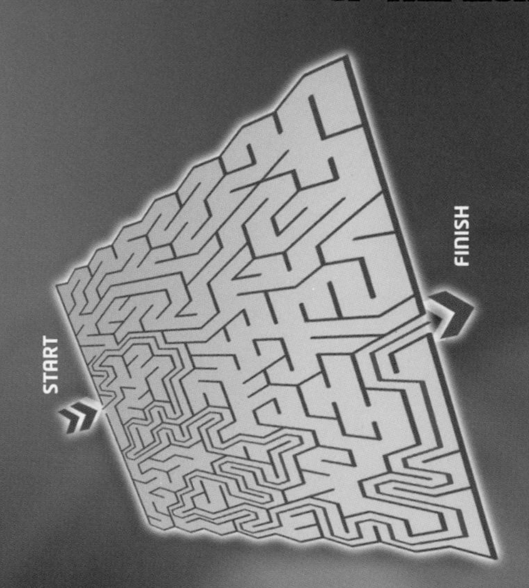

Pg. 10–11
GOLDEN-MOUTHED DROID

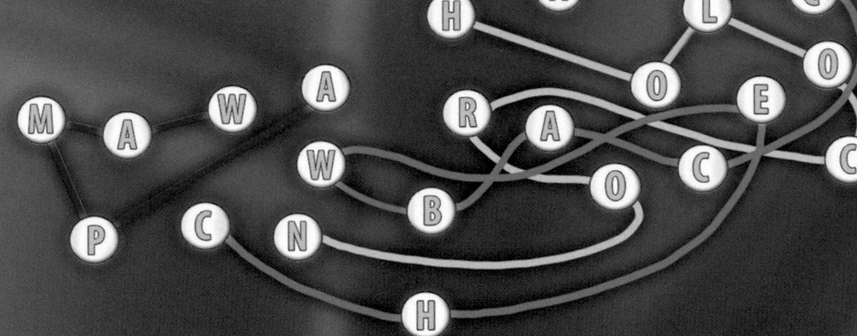

Pg. 14–15
THE SEARCH

258

140
35
60
18
5

D

Pg. 16–17
A NEW CAREER

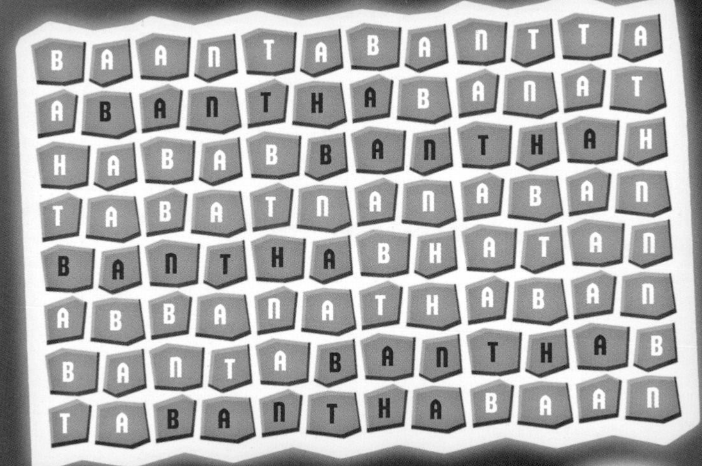

BANTHAS: 

Pg. 18–19 JEDI MASTER

4

Pg. 20–21
LOST IN THE BOG

START

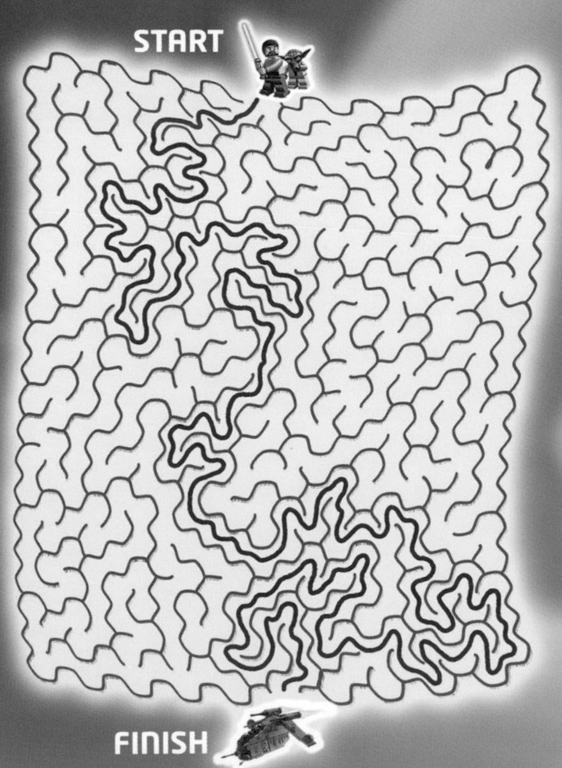

FINISH

Pg. 22–23
FIGHT FOR THE GALAXY

1 2 3 4 5

Pg. 28
SITH SCHEMES

2 4

Pg. 29
ON THE DARK SIDE

7

Pg. 32–33
GALACTIC CROSSWORD

C

3 HUTT

4 SITH

5 C3PO

6 VADER

7 ANAKIN

T

Pg. 34–35
A DREAMER FROM TATOOINE

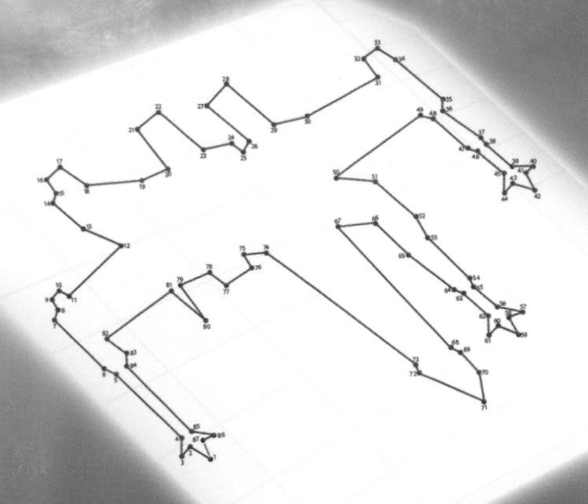

Pg. 36–37
IMPERIAL DESTROYER
TIE FIGHTERS: 17

Pg. 38–39
X-WING ATTACK

Pg. 40–41
HOTH BASE

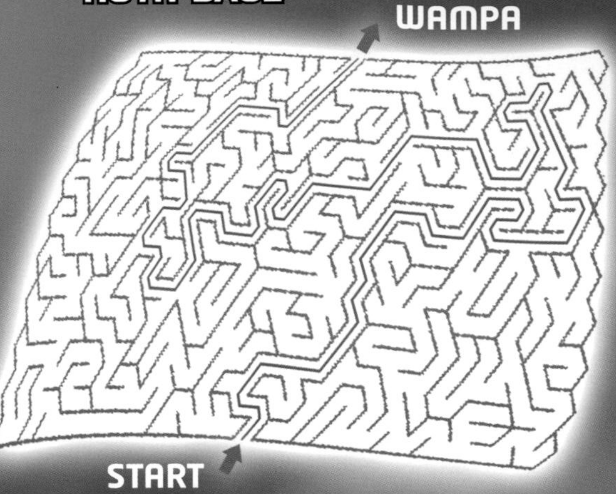

Pg. 42–43
DANCING WITH THE STARS

Pg. 44–45
WEAPON SUDOKU

Pg. 46–47
BATTLE ON HOTH

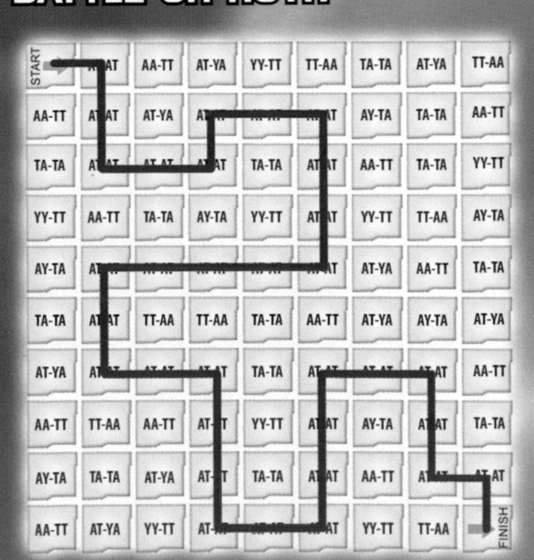